TALES FROM THE ALASKAN GOLD RUSH

JACK R. STANLEY

Wrightbridge Press

*To Mary Lee
with whom all things are possible.*

Tales of the Alaskan Gold Rush

Credits:

Edited by
Mary Lee Stanley
and
Rose Marie Reed

Wrightbridge Press
jacks@wrightbridgepress.com
www.thefictionwritersnotebook.com
www.jackrstanley.com

TWO FREE E-BOOKS

[Murder in Muleshoe]
If you were murdered would they try to find the killer or plan him a parade?

[Guns Along The Rio]
In 1858, two fresh-off-the-ranch 17-year-olds join the Texas Rangers. What could possibly go wrong?

GO TO: http://eepurl.com/dKEi_Y

CHAPTER 1

DANGEROUS CAME
AT KENA

Lodlow "Bitterroot" Rothrock came from Montana to the Alaska Territory, trading one government job for another, not looking for gold. Being from mountains of the Big Sky country had earned him the "Bitterroot" moniker as soon as he bought his first drink in a bar in Anchorage. In those days folks favored handles of that sort over proper names in the gold fields.

Being a man of the wilderness, Bitterroot felt it when he was being watched and followed that day. He knew unseen eyes were on him as he caught a good twenty pound pink fresh water salmon in the Kenai River from the bank. He didn't let his awareness show as he went about his business but he sensed the menace around him.

He was a tad under six feet but muscled with wind-tanned skin and searching black eyes. He wore a full beard that covered the lower part of this round face and hung down to the first button on his coat. Besides his coat he wore knee lace up boots and a flat brimmed hat with a Montana peaked crown.

It was late April,1899, and Bitterroot was on the Kenai Peninsula a good hundred miles south-west of Anchorage on the mostly uncharted land that separated the blue water of the Gulf of Alaska and the Pacific beyond from the waterway called Cook Inlet. The inlet, named after the British navigator and mapmaker, Capt. James Cook, carved a wide and watery path up to Anchorage. But Cook had quickly decided neither the Knik nor the Turnagain Rivers at the inlet's head were the elusive Northwest Passage for which he'd been searching. He had returned to the Pacific and continued his search elsewhere before his death on the shores of Hawaii now a hundred twenty years back.

The Old West "down below" in the states and territories was starting to fade as it saw electric lights and automobiles. But up in the "Great Alone" as many called Alaska, men either walked or rode horses or dog sleds in the winter. Most of men carried a pistol or two, and a Winchester on their saddles.

Coming on late spring as it was, there were still patches of snow in drifts up to a dozen feet clinging to the hillsides and deep shadows. But the days were getting longer and in a month all the snow and ice would be gone.

Bitterroot pitched camp for the night in the woods south of Cooper Landing and cooked his supper.

"Hello the camp!" came the call about a half hour after dark.

"State your business!" Bitterroot called back while chambering a .30-30 round in his '94 Winchester and leveling it in the general direction of the voice.

"'Saw your fire and smelled fish. I have a bag of coffee. Thought we do a little swappin'."

"'Come ahead," Bitterroot said, "but leave your iron on your saddle. I want to see your hands."

"'Wouldn't expect anything less," came the voice again.

A few moments later, the man stepped into the light. He was wearing a faded woolen coat, a strap across his chest and a hunting knife in a scabbard on the belt around the coat. His left hand was open, palm up, while he carried a half rolled paper bag in his right. His hair was saggy brown and grey under the tied up ear flaps of his cap. His face was covered by a gnarled beard that matched his hair. He was average height but on the thin side of lean.

"Welcome," Bitterroot said, lowering his rifle and laying it across his knees. He eased the hammer down. "You're the first man I've come across since I passed Cooper Landing. Name's Rothrock. Lodlow Rothrock. Mostly I go by Bitterroot these days."

"They call me Lonesome," the stranger offered, setting his coffee sack down by the fire.

"'Could I interest you in some fresh-caught salmon?"

"I've never been a man to turn down free food in my life." Lonesome sat on a flat rock directly across from Bitterroot, who was perched on a log with his back against the wide trunk of an ancient Hemlock that towered into the night.

"Help yourself. 'Caught it this morning."

Lonesome took one fillet off a stick slanted into the flames and blew on it before taking a bite.

"You cook good," he said after a moment. "You've added a little to this."

"Thanks. Been seeing to myself for years. But I have to admit this is great salmon up here."

"New comer, are ya?"

"Just off the boat from Seattle less than a month."

"Prospector?"

"Nope. I work for Uncle Sam. I'm doin' a little surveying out here. You?"

"Came up as a stampeder but me and gold don't seem to end up in the same places."

"'Kind of what I expect would be my story if I tried turnin' my hand to gold. A steady pay check is more my line. You can say a lot about the government work, but you can't deny they pay regular."

"'Got me there, friend. I ain't had two dollars to rub together in a year."

"Man that knows his way around can do a lot worse than live off the land."

"True enough --- but winters up here get damned cold."

Bitterroot set his rifle against a big boulder. He started making the coffee, then set it to boil over the fire.

"They call me Bitterroot 'cause I've wintered in the Montana mountains almost a dozen years. Winter ain't my favorite time of year outside, but a man can get used to it and make his way if he's a mind to."

"I do it," Lonesome said, "t' get away from towns and people. I've got me a small cabin nobody knows about but me. I work on it a little every year. Does me right well."

"'Guess that'd be my trouble. No place t' go. When I'm outdoors I spend a lot of time alone like you --- but not for lack of liking people."

"You mean women, I suspect."

"'Course there's that. But I like swappin' tales, playin' cards or checkers. I'm a sociable type, I suppose. By the way, help yourself to all the fish you like, Lonesome, I've had my fill. Tomorrow I'm looking for somethin' bigger. Moose, maybe."

"Moose. That's a tall order. Huntin' and brin'in down a big horn ain't like rabbit or deer."

"Oh, I know. But since I'm up here, I'm going to see what I'm made of --- see if I'm man enough to handle one."

"You never hunted moose in Montana."

"It was always more meat than I wanted to pack. But I decided to give it a try."

"Ever try it without a gun?"

"Big game, you mean?"

"Yup."

"I'm not much of a hand with bow and arrow. I can do okay, but..."

"No. Let me show you something. Put your pistol up on top of that boulder there."

Bitterroot looked at Lonesome curiously a moment, shrugged and stood. He took his Colt from its holster. He thought about it a second more then laid the revolver flat on the crest of the big rock and, taking his seat again, unbuttoned the bottom two buttons of his mackinaw as he did.

Lonesome hadn't moved. He just sat there on the rock.

"The thing about huntin' out here is, what ya' goin'a do when you're out of ammunition? Need money for that. They don't give it away."

"I need to get good with a bow and arrow, is that what you're sayin'?"

"What if you don't have time to get yer bow and arrow ready?"

The night hung silent between them for a moment. Then without any wasted motion, Lonesome snatched a rock about the size of a sourdough biscuit out of the dirt beside him and sailed it like an attacking eagle at Bitterroot's pistol. It struck the revolver frame right over the cylinder and sent the weapon flying off into the dark.

Bitterroot whistled. He was truly impressed.

"Now, that's something I don't know as I could ever do. You actually hunt with just rocks?"

"That and my knives. It's all I've got so I make do."

"How far out can you be that accurate with a rock?

"Near twenty-five sometimes thirty yards, if the wind's right.

"What's the biggest animal you've brought down that'a way?"

"Bear."

"You're joshin' me."

"Black bear. 'Bout five feet tall. 'Weren't no griz."

"I'm thinkin' I'd better stay closer to civilization, Lonesome. You got me worried now."

"I'm just startin'. You ever hear of me?"

"A man named Lonesome? No, can't say I have."

"My real name's Angus Vargo. You should of heard that?"

"Sorry. You famous or somethin'?"

"'Depends on who you ask. 'Ever hear tell of 'the peeler'?"

"The peeler. Isn't that what they call the police in London? That what you mean? "

"No. There's a story about a killer who lives out there on the Kenai. I was glad you were careful when I came up 'cause you never know out here."

"Killer."

"'Likes to sneak up on people, tie'em up, hang'em by their ankles over a low fire, then peel their skin off strip at a time."

"While they're still alive?"

"They say that's what he likes --- hearing'em scream."

"I've heard of Apache's doing that down in Texas, Arizona, and Mexico But a white man?"

"That's what they say."

"Well, somebody ought t' stop him."

"Oh, they've tried, but he's a crafty som'bitch. Catches people unawares."

"From behind, you mean?"

"Mostly. You're sitting backed up to that tree was a good idea."

"You say mostly. He also comes right straight at some?"

"Few. But he's s' quick it don't really matter."

Saying that Lonesome reached up and scratched his shoulder where the strap he wore disappeared down his back. In an instant his hand was over his shoulder and reappeared with a slender dagger he threw at Bitterroot.

Bitterroot jerked to his right while the blade was in the air, grabbing his second revolver from a cross draw holster under the bottom edge of his checkered mackinaw. He got off a single shot before the knife cut into his coat and pinned him against the Hemlock.

Lonesome didn't move even as Bitterroot pulled back the hammer of his single action pistol and prepared to fire again. It was as if they both were frozen in time.

"I can't feel my arms and legs," Lonesome finally said.

Bitterroot ease himself back up and twisted the dagger free, noting blood on its shaft. He kept the pistol trained at Lonesome while he checked under his coat to see his shirt collecting blood from where the cutting edge of the blade had sliced into his shoulder. He would live.

Getting to his feet, Bitterroot stepped to one side of the fire as Lonesome remained exactly where he had been.

"'Think my shot hit you in the neck and must have cut your spinal cord goin' out the back." He took another step behind Lonesome who still hadn't moved. "Yeah," Bitterroot said, "looks like that's what happened."

"You knew who I was all along," Lonesome managed to ask as blood seeped out from between his lips

"I had a pretty good idea somebody was watchin' me all day. Figured if it was you, you'd turn up in the dark. Most cowards work that way."

"Thought you were a government worker. Doin' survey of some kind."

"I am." Bitterroot unbuttoned his coat all the way and pulled it open enough to reveal the badge on his chest. "Alaskan Territorial U.S. Marshall. The survey I'm on is looking for a killer out here on the peninsula. Ten men are missing down here that we know of."

"You were going to be number thirteen."

"Bones have been found but not much else after the bears, wolves and birds get through with them. Now, I know why, Peeler."

"I enjoyed every one of 'em."

"You killin' men just because you could?"

"You have heard of me."

Bitterroot grabbed "the Peeler" by the collar and heaved him forward so that he landed face first in the camp fire. When the criminal screamed but didn't move, Bitterroot snatched him back to a sitting position on his rock, picked up the coffee cup he had used and tossed it on the man's smoldering beard.

"I was just checkin' t' make sure you couldn't move," Bitterroot said, holstering his pistol. "Angus Vargo, you're under arrest for multiple murders --- not that you'll live long enough to stand trial. But somebody can identify you in Cooper Landing or Soldotna. I ain't packing your carcass all the way back to Anchorage. And you should know, that blood coming out of your mouth is also goin' down your windpipe and fillin' your lungs. You're drowning on your own blood."

Bitterroot moved back around to his side of

the fire and stuffed his bandanna on the knife wound on the top of his shoulder under his coat.

The two men sat watching each other across the flames. Blisters were forming on the killer's face.

"If you've got any last words, Vargo, now would be the time to say'em."

Lonesome was silent for a whole minute before he said, "I'm cold." Then his head tilted forward and his body started towards the fire again. Bitterroot was able to lean over and grab the murderer by the shoulder in time to keep him from landing in the coals and flames. He moved Vargo enough so his body dropped to the dirt on his side near the rock on which he had sat.

Bitterroot knelt down the checked Lonesome for a pulse in his neck. There was none. The marshal sighed and stood.

"Where you're goin' you won't be cold long."

The End

CHAPTER 2

THE WINDS OF SKAGWAY

When the late October fog crept up the Northeastern end of the Lynn Canal, the northern most fjord of the Alaska Southeastern panhandle along the Inland Passage, the stampeders, sporting girls, bar keeps, merchants, criminals, and ministers all knew they had less than two hours to finish up any business outdoors. After that they're going to be stormbound from anywhere from a few days to a couple of months. The Alaska panhandle sits at the top of the island waterway that keeps northern British Columbia and the Yukon from touching the Pacific. Skagway is ninety miles Northwest of Juneau. It sits on the flats, carved out by retreating glacial ice. Locals know knew to batten down its wooden shacks and bars, stores, its only hotel and one church, and to button up hundreds of white canvas tents around its muddy streets. The people were aware that what was coming were winds colder than a bitch's tit in a brass brassiere.

The native Tlingit Indians, who would never live in that valley at the mouth of the river, called this place "Skaqua." It means "the place where the North wind blows." Only the white man was so foolish as to erect a town there. But when gold was discovered in the Klondike of Canada's Yukon Territory, the shortest path to get to it was through Skagway. The Chilkoot Pass was right above Skagway and led to Lake Bennett. Those searching for gold would need to get there and then down the raging Yukon River to the town called Dawson.

All those caught on in town or on the trail would have to wait while the Skagway winds raged. Up to seventy miles per hour it blwe and the snow fell horizontally. No man could move more than a few feet under such conditions.

In spite of the damage the gale would inflict and the misery the minus forty below and colder would cause were a time for gold seekers to ready and repair their gear for the struggle ahead. It was also time for the daughters of Eve, the nymphs of the back streets, to make easy money offering the heat of their bodies and the joys of their lost virtue to men of every social strata who sought shelter in the bar and whorehouses along Broadway. It was also a time to tell stories, examine lives, make plans and dream of riches and warmth.

The biggest story in Skagway in the winter of 1898 was the killing of "Soapy" Smith by the town's hero, Frank Reid. Soapy had been a criminal mastermind and unquestioned leader of "The Hundred Thieves." They were his army of con men, card sharps, bunko artists, thugs, ruffians, and crooked officials.

Soapy got his nick name from a scheme he ran in Colorado before heading for the gold fields. He was supposedly selling bars of soap wrapped in $50 and $100 bills. Only Soapy's henchmen ever got the bars with money attached. By the time the suckers realized they'd been taken, Soapy and his men had disappeared from the alley or vacant lot where the sale had taken place.

Except for a starched white shirt, Soapy was always recognized in the black hat, coat, vest, pants, boots and thick matching beard. He was friendly, courteous, quick to laugh and to buy a drink. Unless you'd been one of his victims, chances were that you liked him or at least didn't think him a danger to society. He'd been marshal of the 4th of July parade four days before he was killed.

Frank Reid had once tended bar in one of Soapy's saloons, The Nugget over on Holly. But Frank left to become the town's official surveyor. This was just before Soapy had come to power. Frank kept to himself but the medium built, clean shaven man was known to be no friend of Soapy's. The reasons weren't clear.

All of this was common knowledge in Skagway when the last week of October the fog crept in. It was quickly followed by the North Wind which came screaming between buildings. It whipping under the eaves of buildings, pulling at shingles, boards and windows, while straining the fabrics of every tent still securely staked to the frozen ground.

In the two story Cullen House, a boarding house/hotel at the end of State Street, double fireplaces blazed in the spacious dining room. Even this only managed to keep enough of the chill off the room so the guests could sit. They all hid themselves away at different tables whiling the hours while still seeing their breath. Outside from the assault of the savage wind continued.

Thirty year old newspaper man Doyle Gallant, puffed at his hand carved meerschaum pipe. He was enjoying the company of the slender, yet well endowed, dark haired beauty, Nellie Kane. "The Nightingale of the North," Nellie was a singer.

The lady, it was said, was known to share her charms, privately, on rare occasions, if the price was right. No one thought the lesser of her for this. She, like everyone else in the Klondike, had come to make their fortune using whatever they had. Some had muscles, nerve, courage, cunning, and deceit. Others had looks, perhaps a voice, and all hoped for luck.

Everyone in the Cullen House wore their heaviest winter coats. Nellie Kane was cloaked in a high collar, full length gray otter. The reporter had his fleece lined knee length leather coat.

At the table with them was Brigham Curtis. The beefy, deep voiced owner of Curtis Packers. The company hauled equipment for prospectors on one of his dozen or so strings of mules and pack horses. He was wrapped in an old buffalo robe and laced boots up his calves. Curtis always kept his Montana Peak flat brimmed hat on to keep his completely bald head warm. His round cheeks were permanently red from either sunburn or windburn depending on the season. He spoke from beneath a bushy blond handlebar mustache which drooped past his chin and equally bushy beard.

"Best thing t' ever happen t' this town," he pronounced on the death of Soapy Smith.

"Vigilantes?" the newspaper man Gallant asked.

"Nope. Wish I could say we had somethin' to do with it, but it was all Frank Reid. It was a fair fight."

"Were you a vigilante, Mr. Curtis?" Nellie couldn't believe what she was hearing.

"Proud t' say. The Committee of One Hundred and One we called ourselves. That's one more than Soapy's army of cut throats."

"You took the law into your own hands?" Gallant asked removing his pipe from his mouth.

"Hell, the only other law we had was Deputy Marshal Cotton Weller. Weller had his head so far up Soapy's pocket that when Soapy broke wind,it was Weller who said, 'Pardon me!'" Nellie grinning like a schoolboy who had just said something naughty.

Doyle Gallant scratched his cheek and frowned. The well built reporter thought for a momen. Then he leaned forward asking, "Who was actually on the dock and saw what happened?"

Packer thought, then counted on his fingers. "Jose Siegle, Captain Carl Martin, one of the Hendricks boys, Pierce, I think it was. Plus there was Tommy Lee Hayes, Jess Murphy, J.M. Tanner --- hell, man, there was a bunch."

"What about the stories that it was Jess Murphy who actually shot Soapy?"

"He'd have t' have been one hell of a shot.

Murphy was right outside the door of the shed at the end of the wharf..."

"The Juneau Wharf, correct?"

"Right. We were meeting out there so we'd know who was there and what was said by who. Frank stopped Soapy and his bunch near two hundred, maybe two hundred fifty yards up the planking."

"I understand they both fired at the same time," Nellie said tucking her gloved hands inside the matching muff that lay in her lap.

"That's one of the versions I heard: the reporter said.

"I'll swear I'm right!" Curtis raised his voice. "Then Frank fired twice more. He only had a revolver. Soapy had .44-70 lever action Winchester. "

Doyle Gallant sat back and took a long pull on his pipe before he asked, "Didn't Reid fire one shot that didn't go off?"

Curtis nodded, "Got your facts straight on that. Frank Ried's pistol was a rim fire revolver. Single action. We found one bullet still in the chamber with a rim notch where it had misfired."

"Smith was hit three times in the chest. Once in the heart." The reporter was repeating another of the facts he had heard interviewing others at the time.

"That's a damn lie," Curtis said. "That son of a bitch didn't have a heart."

"And Reid was only shot once --- in the groin," the reporter went on. He glanced at Nellie, "Sorry to be indelicate, Mrs. Kane."

"It's Miss, Mr. Gallant," Nellie said without embarrassment. "I know where the groin is and what it's for."

"Please call me Doyle."

"Doyle. I'm Nellie."

"Everybody knows who you are, Miss Kane," Curtis could tell there was something beginning between his partners at the table.

"It's Nellie to you, too, Mr. Curtis."

"Thank you, ma'am. You're welcome to call me by my first name, but nobody does. Hell, I'm Curtis to everybody."

"Is it true that Soapy Smith's last words were, 'My God, don't shoot?" Nellie asked trying to get back to the story.

"True. He was scared shitless, pardon my French. Frank had caught and held on to the barrel of Soapy's rifle when the S.O.B. tried to bash in ol' Frank's head."

"And Frank Reid was holding on to Soapy's Winchester when it went off?" Doyle wanted to know.

"Yeah, for all the good it did him. Guess that's

why he pumped two more slugs into Soapy as he fell."

"Smith died right there?"

"He was dead before he hit the wharf."

"And Mr. Reid?" Nellie asked after a moment. The only other sounds were the howling of the wind and the crackling of the fireplace across the room from their table by the window.

"Lingered twelve days --- in terrible pain every moment," Curtis said sadly.

"I've seen the monument on his grave," Nellie said. "That was very nice of people to donate for that."

"Biggest funeral Skagway's ever had or ever likely t' have. Two thousand people they say. I didn't count."

"Why is Soapy Smith buried so close to Mr. Reid?" she wanted to know.

"He ain't inside the cemetery. Officially he's three feet outside. If I had my way, we'd a' just tossed his body in the bay --- but Reverend Sinclair said everyman deserves a decent burial. Don't have a guess as to who supplied the dynamite."

"Dynamite?" Nellie wasn't sure she heard Curtis clearly.

"For a grave. All the ground near here is granite. In order to plant someone, first we've got to blow a hole in the rock. We can blast deep enough to put a body in, but they're all standin' up."

"I've never heard of such a thing."

"Nobody's going to spend enough to blow a hole six by three – an' six feet down. They should 'a put Soapy on his head --- so he could see where he was goin'."

"Is it true Smith's body was sprawled on the wharf for a whole day, before it was even moved?" The reporter had been asking around and knew details most people didn't. "I was told that it was only when the next ship docked and people were stepping over his body, that anybody lifted a hand to move him."

"That's a fact. We all took Frank off to try and get him some help. All of Soapy's friends knew what was comin' next. They ran like rats to crawl in their holes or get the hell out of town."

"And what followed was a cleaning out of gamblers, thugs, whores, and the like," Doyle noted.

"We arrested twenty one --- all men. Ever'body knew Soapy was fleecin' the girls on the line, too. If they worked for him, he got half of their money; if they didn't, he found a way to steal it all."

"Why was the U.S. Army called in?" Nellie was remembering what she had been told.

"Well, we weren't the duly appointed law. Soapy had greased so many palms that he had the legal end of everything sewed up. The Army came in because a few of the boys got out of hand and started settin' places on fire. It's hard t' stop sometimes when you've started cleanin' up."

Ma Cullen came over to their table bringing a steaming coffee pot. She was a widow in her 40's, heavy set but with a genuine smile. She was wearing an apron and wiping her free hand on it as she said, "Can I get you folks some coffee?"

"Please," Nellie said and then turned to her companions. "She won't say what her secret is, but Mrs. Cullen makes the best coffee I've ever tasted."

"A girl has to have secrets," she winked. "Miss Kane, you are always a delight. I'm so glad you are here with us again."

"There's no place I'd rather be," Nellie said honestly.

"I agree," Curtis said. "But it's not just her coffee. Everything here is as good as you'll get in Seattle or San Francisco. Believe me, I know," he patted his well rounded belly.

"Never trust a skinny cook," Ma Cullen laughed filling all the cups and looking out the window. "Hope none of you have any plans. I've seen it like this for weeks with no let up."

"Good food, good company, and a wonderful place to sleep, Mrs. Cullen," Doyle smiled.

"They may have to pry me out of here with a crow bar."

"Mr. Gallant, you must have the blarney in you. I knew reporters could write, but you can talk like a silver tongued devil, too." She laughed as she crossed the room to the next table.

The story on Ma Cullen was that she came west with her husband who was murdered. The family robbed before they got to Washington. With two girls to support and no other family or money, Ma Cullen turned to the only profession from which she could make enough to feed herself and her family. She became a whore. She learned the trade, and she opened her own house in Seattle. She was said to have run a clean place and even adopted the children born to the girls who worked for her.

When the gold rush started, she came to Alaska with her brood of nine following the stampeders to start a new life. It hadn't been but a year since she built Cullen House. Running a hotel wasn't as profitable as being a madam, but Ma Cullen was determined to build a legecy so none of her children would ever be forced to make the choice she was once forced to make.

After she had moved on, Curtis said to his companions, "Excuse me a minute." He got to his feet. "There's something I want to show you two." He left in a brisk stride.

Alone Nellie and Doyle sipped their coffee and exchanged looks.

"Why aren't you on the Great White Way, Nellie?" he finally asked.

"You mean what's a nice girl like me ---," she didn't need to finish the thought. "Life," she said and let the single word be her answer.

" I'm serious. You have a lovely voice --- a great figure ---."

"Oh, I know my assets very well. But I'm also a realist. My voice is good --- up here where there's no competition --- but *down below* ...," she said using the term most used to refer to all the other states in the union and the territories, "There are some real singers there --- my pipes are too weak."

She smiled and added, "I barely get across the footlights --- but the men here are so starved for a female voice they'll listen to anything."

"You're short changing yourself."

"No, Doyle, I'm not. I stopped doing that a long time ago. I know who I am and what I can do. I'm making the very best of what I have. When the looks go, and the figure --- and they will ---."

"You are loved, Nellie Kane. Don't you see that in the eyes of your audiences?"

"I see lust, I see --- appreciation, even gratitude. But love? No. If I ever do see that, and in the eyes of a person for whom I really cared ---." She paused and then turned the conversation back on Doyle. "Why are you here?"

"Me?" he sighed. "I used to be a drunk. I could still write pretty well, but I couldn't hold a steady job --- on any paper anywhere. Now that I'm back on my feet --- I have to be on guard everyday not to make the old mistakes. And I don't want to become what many reporters turn out to be --- sad, sour, cynical.. Sometimes I think I've lost the ol' fire in the belly that's supposed to drive us."

"You don't want to get rich?"

"Not anymore. There's just got to be more to this life than money. I'm not sure what that would be, yet, but I'm looking."

She studied his thoughtful eyes before she said, "I've had my disappointments, too, Doyle. I'm no longer welcome in what used to be my home. Or by my family. I'll have to make it on my own --- somewhere. But I've read your work. I've been told they reprint your stories in Seattle and San Francisco -- Boston, Philadelphia --- even New York. That has to please you."

"That's nice but I know the other side of life

down below. I don't want to go back to where I was and what I used to be. I love it here. The energy --- the newness of everything."

"But you have to want to find that one big story --- make a name for myself."

"At times I still do."

"If you find it --- then what?"

"That I don't know. It's something I'm working on while we're hold up. I do know none of us are pure. Take Curtis, for example. He overloads and overworks his horses and mules and then underfeeds them. When they die on the trail, he just heaves their bodies off the road to feed the bears and wolves. Curtis just buys more stock --- cheap. But he has the fever --- get rich at any price. He's fooled himself into thinking he's a kind of Teddy Roosevelt --- the rugged individualist who stands for law and order. How different is he from Soapy Smith? Given the chance would he do the same things?"

"You're a story teller. Ever think about writing novels? Lot of stories here that have never been told."

"Funny you should say that. It's something I've been swishing around in my pan lately. If I find a nugget or even a little color ---. But I also know there's more to Alaska than gold camps and boom towns."

The world paused while the winds raged on and the snow sliced through the air and whited out any view from the window. But Doyle Gallant only saw Nellie Kane.

"Here," Curtis said when he was back, oblivious to what he was interrupting. "Look at this. It's Frank Reid's survey's transit." He handed Nellie the brass mounted metal tube. "This is what Frank laid out Skagway with."

Nellie looked at the instrument and then put it up to her eye and looked out the window.

Handing it to Doyle she said, "I'm afraid I don't know how to use it."

"I don't either," Curtis said, "but it's a piece of history. Frank Reid will always be remembered as the hero of Skagway. If it weren't for him, Soapy Smith and his gang would still have all of us by the throat."

Doyle didn't even attempt to look through the glass but turned the device over examining it.

"Curtis, how well did you know Frank Reid?"

"How well did anybody know him --- we called him 'Quiet man.' Hell, how well does anybody know anybody up here?"

"Did you know he was wanted for murder in Oregon?" Doyle asked.

"I'd heard the story. But how many of us have something we're running away from *down below* ---

or even inside ourselves? The great thing about Alaska is that it's a place for second chances. All of us deserve a second."

"Even Soapy Smith?" Nellie couldn't help but add a barb to the conversation.

"He had his --- and more. Look at what he did with it."

"Who was Nate Clancy?" Doyle asked looking at the instrument still in his hands.

"Never heard of him."

"Oh, I know him," Nellie said. "He's a gentleman. In Dawson City. Family man."

"Surveyor?"

"I believe so, why?"

Doyle pointed to an inscription on the underside of the transit. He read it, "Property of Nate Clancy. He must have come through Skagway on his way up the Golden Stairs." Doyle was referring to the 1,300 steps carved into the icy slope of the Chilkoot Pass. That was where prospectors, who couldn't afford the services of packers like Curtis, had to backpack a total of 1,000 pounds of supplies before the Canadian Northwest Mounted Police would allow them into Canada.

"I don't know? Maybe Frank bought it off of this guy Clancy. Hell, there are men here who would sell their mothers for a chance to get to the fields."

"If --- Clancy had gold fever. Could be he came here to be a surveyor."

"We'll never know," Curtis said with an edge to his voice.

"Oh, I could ask him next time I'm in Dawson," Doyle said casually relighting his pipe.

"You leave it along, damn you!"

"Curtis, why does it matter to you? Don't you want to know the truth?"

"Truth according to who?"

"So, Frank Reid managed to --- let's say 'obtain' --- Nate Clancy's surveyor tools. And suddenly he becomes the surveyor of Skagway," Doyle thought out loud. "It certainly would explain how Captain Moore lost his land."

Former riverboat captain William "Billy" Moore was the very first settler on the flats by Skagway Bay. He staked out 160 acres, built a cabin, and scouted the trail up the Chilkoot Pass to the Yukon River in 1877. Ten years later, Frank Reid produced a new survey of what had been Mooresville but became Skagway. Suddenly Captain Moore's cabin was right in the middle of the main street. Captain Moore lost his land and title --- until it would be upheld by a Federal court still five years later in 1897 --- last year.

Curtis snatched the transit out of Doyle's hands and leapt to his feet.

"He died for Skagway. I won't sit here and listen to anyone dishonor Frank Reid."

"Could be Frank Reid did what he did to himself," the reporter said evenly. "Of course, if you happen to know he wasn't a real surveyor all along...." Doyle let the question hang in the air.

Without another word, Curtis turned and stalked off, his heavy boots pounding the hardwood floor as he went.

"You've not made a friend there," Nellie said.

"'And ye shall know the truth and the truth shall set you free.' So says the Good Book."

"Are you going to print that story?" she asked.

"I'd have to go back to Dawson and talked to Nate Clancy, first. Even then ... Just because something is true is no reason it should be shouted from the roof tops. Frank Reid did a good thing in spite of who he might have been before. Why shouldn't he be remembered for that instead of all the rest? Most of us would rather not have our good deeds 'interred with our bones' to misquote the bard."

"And if this is your 'big story'?"

Doyle thought for a moment before he said, "If this is true, I won't be the only one to discover it. I think I'll let someone else tell this story."

Nellie Kane smiled at Doyle Gallant. "I think

you've earned your name, Mr. Gallant. You're a good man."

"Those are warm words on a very cold afternoon. Thank you, Nellie, I won't forget them."

She reached out a gloved hand and took one of his in hers.

Then as the Skagway winds wailed, Nellie and Doyle shared their warmth and her bed with the newspaper man. They would continue to do so until the storm relented three weeks later. But then it was time for them to go their separate ways.

Nellie Kane found her gold and ended her says as a socialite in San Francisco. Doyle Gallant stayed in "the great alone" and wrote stories both factual and fictional and became a legendary Alaskan man of letters. Brigham Curtis is lost to history as are most of those who are takers and think of themselves before anyone else. Soapy Smith is remembered for the dastardly cur he was and Frank Reid is still revered where the winds of Skagway blow and tales of daring deeds are told.

THE END

CHAPTER 3

KLONDIKE JUSTICE

L anky Ed "Longstory" Fields didn't figure he had a Chinaman's chance of defending "Fair Deal" Doak Logan for the murder of "Quicksilver" Riggs DeGraf. First off, Longstory was a barber by trade. He had read about lawyers, like Portia, the disguised heiress in Shakespeare's Merchant of Venice, Sydney Carton in A Tale of Two Cities, stories of Abraham Lincoln, and others. Ed Fields got the handle "Longstory" 'cause he read a lot and seemed to remember every word when he retold the stories. Problem was, none of them seem to help when they were needed.

It was January, 1901 in Circle City, an Alaska gold rush boomtown on the upper reaches of the Yukon River, a good hundred miles northeast of

Fairbanks. His Honor, chunky and squint-eyed "Lucky Cajun" Gustave Thibodeaux, sounded like a lawyer and claimed he was one – once. That was before he killed a man in a New Orleans duel and headed as far North as he could go for the sake of his health. After he was unanimously elected to be the judge for a "miner's court," the Lucky Cajun seated "a baker's dozen of sober men" to be the jury as a true miner's court required. He also appointed "Stagestruck" Jim Nell as prosecutor, because the handsome, pencil-mustached actor had a wonderful voice and when drunk often broke into Shakespearean soliloquies. Only Stagestruck enjoyed hearing himself talk more than the soiled doves of Circle City. The Lucky Cajun thought Jim Nell would play the part well.

Longstory was about the only person beside Effie Washburn who really believed gambler Doak Logan hadn't shot the victim. You cut a man's hair a few time, you get to know him. Longstory thought of Fair Deal as neat, methodical, courteous—but certainly not a killer.

These days Longstory was doing what he knew best, barbering while he bided his time for the right chance to take another load of supplies up the Chilkoot Pass. He was only a hundred and fifty pounds shy of the thousand pounds the

Mounties required for anyone headed for the Canadian Klondike gold fields.

Shaving and currying the stampeders looking for gold, or a way to make a buck off those who had some, wasn't a particularly profitable job. Most men in the gold fields like to keep the mane on their heads and their faces to fend off the cold. It was mostly shopkeepers, bartenders, and gamblers who were his regular customers. But his shop, really just a room in the back of The Alaskan saloon, soon became a good place to hang around and hear a story of a book or play the barber had read.

When the Lucky Cajun cast Longstory as Fair Deal's defense attorney, nobody gave the barber a hot coal's chance in a whiteout blizzard of saving Doak from being the main attraction at a neck stretching before the day was over. Longstory, however, had an idea and if he could get just one of his customers to come forward with a little information here and there, Doak still might see another sunrise without a set of wings or a pitch fork as a door prize. Folks liked Doak and didn't much give a damn for Quicksilver when he was alive.

Still, all bets were off when the curtain went up on this little drama. Stagestruck was good at making up his own lines and making them sound like they not only belonged in the script he was either quoting or performing. So as a prosecuting attorney Longstory couldn't expect every word out of the actor's mouth to be the truth.

Everybody was making this tale up as they went. Even if Longstory was on the right side of the truth he wasn't sure how good he was going to be at the improvisation of a trial.

Things didn't go right from the outset. The problems started with the closing down the Golden Mecca saloon for the few daylight hours in the depth of a hard winter. That made a lot of stampeders mad. There were only four hours when the sun was over the horizon at that time of year. And the Golden Mecca, the biggest bar in town, was known to be the cleanest and most honest houch house around. It didn't sell any watered-down liquor and boasting the prettiest whores for two hundred miles. But it was also the only place with enough space for a miner's court, witnesses, and gawkers. Everu Tom, Dick and jackass from the Arctic Circle to Seattle would be talking about for the next year. Nobody wanted to miss it.

Longstory also knew that sober and angry prospectors didn't tend to say much, especially if talking stood between them and getting the bar opened. So, getting good testimony could be a real chore.

Then there was the fact that the trial wasn't really legal because no one had the authority or the jurisdiction to hold a tribunal much less render a verdict and carry it out. Justice is often an unknown quantity on the frontiers and in boomtowns. Law and order exists more in men's minds that in reality. This kangaroo court, however, could and would serve up a long drop to a man tied to a short rope if it decided to—and there was nobody to stop it.

Everybody who knew the recently departed, Quicksliver Riggs DeGraf, for more than three minutes would have had a reason to blow Quicksilver's quarrelsome brains out. Fair Deal's problem as the accused was that he and Quicksilver had words over a poker game in the Elmont Saloon just three days before Quicksilver went missing. Dapper little Fair Deal had produced a four barreled pepperbox sleeve Derringer at the peak of the disagreement before Quicksilver could get his Remington hog leg out of his holster.

Fair Deal was just five feet seven and only about 90 pounds even with ice-caked mukluk boots on. Quicksilver had been six two, two hundred sixty pounds with full fiery red beard. But that pepperbox would have made mush of Quicksilver's bulbous nose and even with his mercurial temper raging, the hulking, luckless prospector knew when to step back. The whole saloon was silent and even Longstory, who was there at the time, heard Quicksilver's famous last words.

"All right, gambler, but if anything happens to me, everybody here will know who to look for!" He snatched up what was left of his poke from the table and stomped out of the bar.

Doak uncocked his pistol and slipped it back up his sleeve while the other players slapped him on the back and Longstory told him to watch his step on the way home.

Nobody trusted Quicksilver, but Fair Deal had a solid reputation. He was a gambler, but he had lost big pots and had long runs of bad luck when no card would turn right for him. He had given grubstakes to prospectors and been staked into games when he didn't have a particle of gold dust to his name. He was as quick with a smile and a joke as Quicksilver was with his ill temper.

Everybody also knew Fair Deal was sweet on Effie Washburn, the most sought-after girl in the Klondike. Effie, renowned across the Klondike simply as, "The Beauty," made no pretense about what she did for a living. But she was both picky and expensive to those fortunate enough to taste her delights. She was five feet six herself, slender with a delicate, peaches and cream complexion, a lovely smile, and an iron will. She always dressed like a lady in floor length, high collar dresses with her hair swept up into a bun on the top of her head, giving her a profile just waiting to be immortalized in a cameo.

The Beauty worked out of the Golden Mecca of which she owned half. The other half was owned by Uncle Cecil Hoffman. Cecil, a man of about 50, came up a couple of times a year and took the Mecca's profits back to bank and to invest in Seattle for both The Beauty and himself. Longstory didn't know if Cecil was really Effie's uncle or if that was just his nickname—but it wasn't the kind of question anyone in the Klondike asked.

Those who Effie had favored with her passion all had clean shaven faces, baths and new clothes. In a boom town like Circle, these men always stood out. They were proud to be unique and some were proud of how much they had been willing to spend for a night with Effie. It was always thousands of dollars, but only the most successful stampeders had the wherewithal to make such an investment, and they were happy to part with whatever they paid. It was often said that some delighted in paying more than those in the past. The closest Longstory ever got to being one of The Beauty's select, was in being the one who shaved the lucky men's faces.

It was ironic that Fair Deal's trial was held in the Mecca because he never went there for business, only the pleasures of The Beauty, for which he alone did not have to pay. She sat in the first row of chairs behind Fair Deal and Longstory and cried often as the evidence unfolded.

The facts were that Quicksilver had been found on Short Bluff sixty-five feet above a bend in the Yukon River. There was a big hole in his head where his brains had been. When he was found, his intelligence was mostly a frozen bloody mass on the trail beside the body which had also become a solid block of ice a couple of hours after his last breath. His poke was gone, and so was his pistol, his only two possessions as far as anyone knew. No murder weapon was located and it looked like his prediction had come true; Fair Deal had murdered Quicksilver after the surly no- account had been turned down flat by The Beauty whom he slapped to the floor before he left the Golden Mecca.

Word quickly reached Fair Deal who left a winning hand and a rather decent-sized pot to rush to Effie. After he went upstairs to The Beauty, he wasn't seen again for a day and a half. It was assumed Fair Deal took the back stairs out of the Mecca, located Quicksilver and sent the son of a bitch to hell, where he belonged.

Fair Deal and Beauty claimed to have been together the whole time and she had had to sit on him to keep him from going after Quicksilver. The prosecutors grinned at each other imagining The Beauty was most likely naked when she sat astride Doak. Still, Quicksilver had turned up dead, and murder was almost as bad as claim-jumping to the stampeders. There had to be a trial.

When The Beauty took the stand, she was questioned gently by Longstory wearing his trademark brown and white mackinaw and fur flap-eared hat.

"Effie, would you lie for Doak Logan to keep him from hanging?"

"I don't lie for anybody." Then as an afterthought she added, "In the case of Fair Deal, I don't have to. And before you ask, no, he didn't ask me to lie for him. If he had, the answer would have been, 'No.'"

"There's no one in Circle who doesn't know you and your high standards. What was it about Quicksilver that caused you to tell him, 'No!'?"

"Mr. DeGraf was no gentleman. I have neither time nor affection for any man who is not a gentleman."

"Are you saying this because he struck you?"

"I'm saying it because it is the truth."

The Golden Mecca shook with applause. Longstory had made a good point and he knew it. Effie was going to be his best witness.

"Was Fair Deal with you from the time he came to your room until you two were seen together down here a day and a half later?"

"Yes."

Longstory returned to his chair telling the court, "No more questions."

"It's your turn, Stagestruck," the Lucky Cajun said to the prosecutor who was mostly focused on how he looked – and he did look like a lawyer, the judge admitted to himself.

Stagestruck stood to his full six feet and took a deep breath so he would be in good voice before he stepped onto center stage.

"Friends, Alaskans, Canadians. The prosecution comes not to praise Quicksilver DeGraft, but to bury Fair Deal Doak Logan for his crime of murder. We have but one question for this witness," he said as if the whole trial turned on this single inquiry. "How can you be positive that Doak Logan did not slip away from you in the night, steal down the back stairs, and dispatch Quicksilver by blowing his brains out?"

Effie let a small Mona Lisa smile paint her lips before she calmly said, "First, I'm not sure Riggs DeGraf had any brains and secondly, – one way or the other – Doak was between my legs–all the time."

The Golden Mecca exploded in roars and

laughter. It took the Cajun a full minute of pounding on the table to bring the room back under control.

As soon as The Beauty could be heard over the diminishing noise, she continued, "Thus, every time he moved, I was aware of it."

Stagestruck was smart enough when it was time to exit. He sat down without another word.

"Thank you, Miss Washburn," the Lucky Cajun said trying with all his might not to laugh. "You may step down. Next witness, Longstory."

"Doak Logan," the defense attorney called, trying very hard to play his part but afraid his client, honest gambler or not, might not come off as well as Effie.

Fair Deal stood and walked the few steps to the witness chair where he took an oath to tell the truth and sat down.

"Well, I have but one question for you, Doak," Longstory said. "Did you kill Quicksilver Riggs DeGraf?"

Scanning the crowd, and then sighing before he spoke, Fair Deal said, "I wish I had—but I didn't. I wasn't afraid of Quicksilver, but Effie begged me to let him go. She has a way of getting what she wants." He turned to look at her as he said, "I never want to disappoint her. That's the only reason I didn't go after him."

Looking back at the crowd he finished with, "I'm glad somebody did him in—but it wasn't me."

Longstory took his seat.

Stagestruck was shaking his head when he finally got up.

"For the life of me, I cannot conjure any method to inquire of this witness and know definitively he wasn't fabricating some elaborate prevarication."

Many a miner turned to those next to him for a translation of Stagestruck's comment.

"He thinks Doak will be lying no matter what he says," Longstory paraphrased for the crowd.

To answer Stagestruck, Doak said, "I swore to tell the truth, and I have."

"You also said you wished you had killed Quicksilver."

"I did."

"It's not a big leap from wishing to doing."

"How many men in this room," Longstory cut in, "wish they had already struck it rich but they never have?"

Again there was laughter.

"No questions," Stagestruck finally said, dropping back to his chair.

"Any other witnesses?" the Lucky Cajun drawled.

Longstory looked around the room searching

for someone who knew something he didn't. But thought perhaps Doc Cody might help but Doc just looked away. Did the camp's only doctor know something? Doc was one of a handful of professionals who had hang out a shingle in Circle after several hard, luckless years in the territory. He like many he finally decided he was never going to make it as a prospector. But neither Doc nor anyone else spoke up saying they were willing to testify. Longstory knew he had done all he could do, as little as that was.

"No more witnesses," Longstory said in a defeated tone.

The Lucky Cajun called for final arguments by the prosecution and the defense. It was clear Stagestruck was the better performer. He strutted, posed, and with his booming voice, affected way of speaking, and a little logic, he soon had not just the jury, but the whole crowd in his hand. He depicted Fair Deal as an almost admitted killer who was hiding behind the skirts of The Beauty.

Longstory tried to turn things around but he was no thespian, much less a lawyer. Since no one else had volunteered any information, all he had to rely on were the words of Effie and Doak. Longstory was a storyteller, not a debater, and try as he might he couldn't make this tale come out the way he wanted. He was on the ropes and he hated it. Stagestruck had swung most everyone in the saloon to his way of thinking. When Longstory finally slumped in his chair he felt he had let Effie, Doak, and himself down. There was no one else to give Doak an alibi and his lawyering wasn't panning out.

Folks were still crowding into the room when the Cajun told the jury to go and deliberate. The fourteen men looked at each other as they stood, and all shook their heads.

"Arkansas Jim" Aberdeen was jury foreman. The pock marked faced sourdough turned and sat back down along with the others.

"Lucky," Arkansas Jim said to the judge, "we don't need to deliberate."

"Then, members of the jury," the Cajun announced in a very formal voice, "what say you in the matter of Doak Logan versus Riggs DeGraf? Do you find Fair Deal guilty or not guilty?"

Longstory had his head in his hands because he knew what was coming. But before Arkansas Jim could open his mouth Doc Cody jumped to his feet in the middle of the crowded saloon and shouted, "Just a damn minute!"

Longstory couldn't believe his ears. This was what he had been hoping for. If Doc would say something, others might follow.

"Before anything crazy happens here, I've got

to say something." Doc Cody's clear grey eyes were on fire in a face mostly covered by salt and pepper hair and beard.

"Point of order," Stagestruck intoned a hand gripping each lapel of his black coat. "The prosecution and the defense have rested and the matter is now in the hand of our esteemed jury."

"Shut the hell up, Stagestruck!" the Cajun shot back. "This is a courtroom. My damn courtroom! And I decide what is proper and what isn't."

"Your honor," Stagestruck protested.

"Sit down, Stagestruck!" the Lucky Cajun roared. "We're not goin' to hang anybody until everybody's had their say. Go ahead, Doc, what have you got?"

Doc Cody took off his bowler hat and ran a bony hand through his unruly hair.

"Everybody here knows me and knows I keep secrets."

All around the room men and women glanced down not wanting to meet Doc's eyes. Longstory almost winced recalling the boils on his butt Doc had lanced and promised to neither laugh about or tell anyone.

"But I ain't going to stay quiet when I know something and it makes a big difference. Quicksilver Riggs DeGraf didn't come here looking for gold. He'd been to every doctor and medicine man in the Klondike, and I was the last one. I told him the same thing all the rest had. That is that he was dyin'."

This stirred the crowd. Longstory looked at Doak and Effie. There was a gleam of hope in their eyes again.

"He had a cancer growin' inside of him," Doc Cody went on, "and there was no way to cut it out or cure it. Just like his bad temper, it was eating him alive."

"How do we know that, Doc?" the Lucky Cajun asked. "No offense, but we only have your word for this."

"Wait until spring break-up and his body thaws out enough for an autopsy. I'll cut him open, and you can all see."

Break-up was the time each spring when the frozen river finally cracked and began to flow again. The exact hour and minute the Yukon River would begin moving again and taking out the only bridge in Circle across the water was the biggest betting pool each spring.

"And what do we do until June?" Stagestruck wanted to know? "Let Logan go if he'll promise not to leave town?"

This got a good laugh from the crowd.

"You can't hang Doak until you know for sure," Longstory demanded.

"What Doc says is true." A tiny voice seeped through the rumble.

"Who said that?" the Lucky Cajun wanted to know.

"I did," petite Corrine Warner said. Called "The Virgin," Corrine was the youngest fairy on the Yukon - fairies being one of the nicer euphemisms for women who made their living watching the ceiling while miners mined the ladies virtue. She was nicknamed not because of her age or state of chastity, but because one stampeder had joked that Corrine might have actually seen a virgin before she came north. The name stuck. The Virgin worked out of The Extraordinaire, two blocks away and she got top dollar for her services. Not the kind of money paid to The Beauty, but her collection of nuggets was said to rival any sporting woman's in the gold fields.

"Quicksilver came to see me, cussin' Effie up a blue streak. 'Must have been right after she turned him away."

"You didn't turn him away, did you, Virgin?" Stagestruck had to find a way back into the center of attention.

The Virgin balled her little fists and planted one on each hip. "I came up here for the same reason all the rest of you did: to get rich. I don't turn anybody away. You should know that

Longstory." The room exploded into laughter and applause.

After Longstory recovered from the jab, he asked, "What did Quicksilver tell you that corroborates what Doc is saying?" the Cajun asked over the crowd. Longstory thought to himself that he needed to remember the word "corroborates." It sounded very lawyerlike.

The room fell silent as The Virgin said, "He said he hurt all the time and couldn't take it much longer."

"I'm afraid this is mere hearsay and not evidence," Stagestruck blurted. "Unless there is more proof than that ...."

"Is it proof that he couldn't get it up," the Virgin spoke up, "and that he left without taking his poke with him?"

"How much was in his poke?" Stagestruck demanded.

"Just enough to cover my services," The Virgin said with a straight face.

"More than he left inside The Virgin," one stampeder yelled.

"Sounds like Quicksilver," another joked. "He couldn't get a poke, so he left his poke!" Again the room was rocking with laughter.

"Not being able to get it up," Doc Cody said

when the room had settled down, "and being in constant pain are both side effects of his cancer."

"Circumstantial evidence at best," Stagestruck proclaimed, back in charge again. "If Quicksilver had taken his own life, his big pistol should have been right there beside his body."

Effie and Doak now looked at each other defeated. Longstory felt like a warm pile of moose dropping. He wasn't helping Fair Deal at all.

From the back of the room a rough voice sounded with a foreign accent. "What did his pistol look like?"

"He carried a .44 Remington - Russian." The Lucky Cajun was on his feet now and trying to locate the speaker.

"Like this?" a bulky prospector with a fur cap and ear flaps along with a pipe between his stained teeth spoke as he worked his way forward through the crowd. He held a large handgun.

He handed the weapon to the Cajun who nodded his head as he examined it. "This looks to be Quicksilver's—except for the broken hammer. Who are you and where did you get this?"

"I am Kirk Nerland. From Norway. Here two weeks only so far. I find this fishing."

"Fishing? This time of year?" Stagestruck was sure he had caught the man in a lie.

"Ice fishing," the stampeder answered. "Like we do in Norway."

"Fishing where?" It was Longstory anxious for some good news for a change.

"Third turn in the river. East of town."

"Below Short Bluff?"

"I don't know what it is called," Nerland said.

"Was there a bluff, a cliff there?"

"Jes," said Nerland. "But I was fishing out in the river."

"What happened to the hammer of this fine firearm?" Stagestruck asked.

"That is how I found it—only tied to a big rock."

"Tied with what?"

"Rope."

"How long a rope?"

Nerland looked around and pointed to where Arkansas Jim sat with the rest of the jury. "From here to there."

"Fifteen feet," Longstory calculated.

"Why in hell would somebody tie Quicksilver's gun to a rock and throw it in the river? It makes no sense." Stagestruck was trying to thrill the audience with his voice again.

"It did if somebody didn't want that gun found," Longstory said half to himself. "But why fifteen feet of rope?"

There was a discussion of many voices until the

Lucky Cajun banged on his table and called for silence.

"Any idea?" he finally asked.

"The rope and the gun–they weren't in the water. On top of it–covered only with snow and some ice.

"Let me see that pistol," Longstory said stepping over and picking up the .44. "It took a lot of force to break this hammer."

"It wasn't broken when he came to see me," Doc Cody said.

"I don't remember seeing it broken either," the Virgin added.

"Does anybody else remember that chip out of the boulder near Quicksilver's body?" Longstory looked around hopefully.

"Yeah," Leo King, known around town as Big Tooth (although few called him that to his misshapen face) He spoke from the audience. It had been Leo who had first come across Quicksilver's frozen remains. "I remember wondering if that had anything to do with a fight Quicksilver might have had with whoever killed him."

"What if ---," Longstory was getting an idea and his eyes flashed as he put the pieces together, "--- what if Quicksilver tied his own gun to that rock so after he shot himself, the rock would fling this pistol into the river. About fifteen feet would have put the weight of that rock on the other side of the boulder and with no one holding the .44, the rock would have yanked the gun and flipped it over onto the frozen river."

"Absolutely preposterous!" Stagestruck bellowed. "Let us not destroy a dead man's good name with such an unlikely supposition."

"Quicksilver—a good name?" Longstory asked and laughter showered the room.

"All right, I will withdraw that statement," Stagestruck took up his best pose as he continued, "but please, gentlemen, we are here for justice and not for tall tales. There is no way to prove Quicksilver killed himself and went to elaborate means to cast the blame for his demise on Fair Deal. May it please the court, the jury was about to announce its verdict. I respectfully ask to hear that verdict."

"I can't let this happen again!" It was "Beaver" McClemmey, a fuzzy faced giant with a raspy voice.

This was the miracle for which Longstory had been hoping. He knew what Beaver was going to say, but it wasn't the barber's story to tell, even if it had meant Doak's life. Beaver had shared it with Longstory in confidence. A barber may not be a priest or professional man, but Longstory was not a man to violate a trust. If word had gotten out that Beaver was talking, Quicksilver might have gone hunting for the prospector.

Everybody in Circle knew Beaver. One of the hardest luck stampeders, he'd come up overland through the Chilkoot Pass in '97 to Dawson City in the Yukon, only to find all the claims worth a damn already staked. He struggled back to Seattle only to come back for the next rush in 1900, this time taking the longer route from Nome down the Yukon River. All the gold he ever found was just enough to keep him alive.

Beaver was a hardworking man. He had hauled and dug for wages from some off the biggest winners and biggest losers in the Klondike. He was known these days as a bouncer at The Eldorado. At six feet six and three hundred fifty pounds of muscle, he was a man who miners trusted with their money. Many a miner would come into town, find Beaver and entrust him with the prospector's poke while the man went out to see the pink elephants. Days or even weeks later the recovering stampeder would locate Beaver again and get their poke back only as they boarded a boat home.

"Beaver," the Cajun asked, "what'd you say?"

"I can't let this happen again."

"What happen?"

"This ain't the first time Riggs DeGraf blamed somebody else. In '98 he did the same thing over in Eagle."

"I demand we hear the verdict!" Stagestruck pouted.

"We'll get the verdict when I'm damn good and ready," the Cajun sounded on edge, "and not before! Go ahead, Beaver."

"Back in '98 Riggs told a crowd in the streets of Eagle that if anything happened to him, folks should look to 'Whiskey' Callahan, who, half drunk, had just whooped Quicksilver's ass in a fair fight. Well, a week later Riggs had vanished. All his gear was still on his worthless claim, but there was no sign of Riggs. A mob hung Whiskey." Beaver paused here, took a deep breath and said, "I was in that mob."

No one in the Mecca could believe it. Beaver was respected and even loved, and it was hard to believe he was anything but a saint.

"When I first saw him here in Circle, I jerked him up by the collar and asked him what he had done. He said he just decided to leave Eagle and didn't do a damn thing wrong. If anybody was wrong, he said, it was fools like me who hung an innocent man, not him. Now, the son of a bitch is doing it again."

Longstory turned back to the jury.

"We know what kind of man Quicksilver was—vengeful and malicious ---. He was in pain from the cancer that was killing him, but there is no proof that Fair Deal even saw Quicksilver after the poker game in the Elmont. Effie Washburn has told you Fair Deal never left her once he got to her side the night she told Quicksilver, 'No'.

"You boys know Fair Deal. Is he the kind of man to shoot someone like Quicksilver and then set up an elaborate way to hide it? Or was Quicksilver the sort who would gladly shift the blame for his own suicide to someone he hated so he could laugh about it in hell? You've heard from Doc, The Virgin, and from Beaver. Now, who are you going to believe?"

The Lucky Cajun asked the jury, "Do you want to deliberate now?"

The men huddled together, some leaning backwards in their chairs, some standing. A moment later Arkansas Jim stood up. "We know our verdict."

"Let's have it," the Lucky Cajun said.

"We find Fair Deal not guilty."

"Case dismissed, court adjourned!" the Lucky Cajun declared as he banged the bund hole hammer on the table. "The bar's open!"

A cheer went up from the crowd and The Beauty grabbed Longstory, giving him a kiss he never forgot.

---o---

Arkansas Jim, the foreman of the jury, found and lost three fortunes before he became a preacher. His message was always the one thing he took away from Fair Deal's trial, the importance and power of forgiveness.

The Lucky Cajun got his wish of dying a rich man. He struck it rich in '03 only to have claim jumpers swoop down on his mine early one July morning. He and his crew beat back the attacking gang, and the Cajun killed the bastard who had fired three shots into the Cajun's chest. The Lucky Cajun never felt any pain, never realized he was shot. He just suddenly felt a tiredness come over him before he slumped to the ground dead. Still, when he died, the Lucky Cajun was a rich man. The fortune he left made him the savior of his almost destitute family back in Louisiana. He was revered and remembered.

Doc Cody couldn't resist the lure of prospecting and hit his mother lode in the save rush of '03 at Nome. What he discovered after a 'round the world cruise and anything money could buy was that he was happiest doing something that made a difference, like being a physician. He used his money to open a hospital in Anchorage where he practiced his healing arts until the day he died.

Beaver McClemmey married The Virgin, Corrine Warner, and using her money and his reputation, opened The Miners Bank of Alaska. They became civic leaders and the very top of Fairbanks' polite high society.

Kirk Nerland, whose ice fishing hole found Quicksilver's Remington .44, found his fortune not in gold but in the salmon fishing business. He lived out his days in Ketchikan along the Alaska Southeast Inland Passage.

Fair Deal left the Klondike with The Beauty and Uncle Cecil Hoffman, who turned out to be Effie's real uncle. The investments Uncle Hoffman had made led Effie and Doak to gamble on the wine business in northern California. There they founded a dynasty which continued long after Effie, Doak and the trial were lost to history.

And Longstory? He never forgot that kiss from The Beauty—and it changed his life. He made it to Dawson but had already decided good things could come from being an attorney. He did a little prospecting but more hair cutting and began to study the law. He became a lawyer and eventually went to Congress to represent the territory of Alaska. And that kiss? He remembered it as he took the oath to become territorial governor.

By anybody's reckoning, justice had come out of Circle City and the Klondike in 1901.

THE END

TWO FREE E-BOOKS

[*Murder in Muleshoe*]
**If you were murdered would they try to find
the killer or plan him a parade?**

[*Guns Along The Rio*]
**In 1858, two fresh-off-the-ranch 17-year-olds
join the Texas Rangers. What could possibly
go wrong?**

GO TO: http://eepurl.com/dKEi_Y

Incdennt At Lajitas

Jack R. Stanley

INCIDENT AT LAJITAS

Former Texas Ranger Clay Maxwell wanted nothing more than to be left alone to live his life in Del Rio, Texas. He was tired of doing other men's dirty work and killing every young gunslinger looking to make a name for himself. Nothing could get him to go back to doing what he does best. Yet when Lord Wilford Bristol's prize stallion is stolen by Mexican Comancheros, Maxwell's answer to retrieving the horse was, "Yes." He got a group of hardened professionals together, and they cross the Rio Grande. These men, along with Lord Bristol's foreman, Tom Kelso, were the only men who'd agree to go into hell to get back the animal.

GET IT AT AMAZON
Print
Large Print
Ebook

ABOUT THE AUTHOR

Jack R. Stanley is an award-winning novelist, playwright, and screenwriter. As an officer and combat photographer in Vietnam, he earned the Bronze. He earned both his M.A. and his Ph.D. at the University of Michigan in Ann Arbor in Radio-TV-Film. His doctoral dissertation was on the TV series GUNSMOKE. Still married to his gifted high school sweetheart, Stanley was TV Area Head at The University of Texas at Austin's Department of Radio-TV-Film. He later moved to deep-south Texas and the Lower Rio Grande Valley for a challenging position with The University of Texas-Pan American. Here he taught Theatre-TV-Film for 30 years in the Department of Communication serving as Department Chair at U.T.P.A. for 11 years. He now lives in the Texas Panhandle where he writes his fiction. His webpage is www.-jackrstanley.com.

ALSO BY JACK R. STANLEY

ALSO BY THE AUTHOR

Novels

[Westerns]

Guns Along The Rio

West Of The Frio

A Hard Line Between The Rios

The Mormon Marshal

Along The Outlaw Trail

The Gavel and the Gun

13 Steps To Hell

Incident At Lajitats

Pancho's Pilot

Return to Redemption

Occurrence At Latigo

The Hussy and the Hardcase

Ode To An Outlaw

[Science Fiction]

A New War

Between Love And Murder

Blood Drive

Death Scene

The Defection of Grigori Dorsky

The Evil Eye

Fatty and Hearst

Gideon: The Horse That Saved Texas

Hell In Paradise

Hollowpoint

Holiday For An Assassin

Horse Thief Hollow

Incident A tLajitas

Love, Lust, & Life

Mom & Apple Pye

Pancho's Pilot

The Prometheus Peril

The Rape of Sarah Quinn

Reservations

River of Tears

Seven Reasons Why

The Thing About Love

The Texas Rattlesnake Murders

Too Good To Be True

The Vampire Rose

A Violent End

The Virgin Casanova

Plays

Antigone In Texas

Cyrano

The Last Virgin From Las Vegas

The Seven Keys

The Unwed Widow

www.ingramcontent.com/pod-product-compliance
Lightning Source LLC
Chambersburg PA
CBHW070645130626
46555CB00006B/2717